TABLE OF CONTENTS

FOR MRS. BISHOP, THE TOWN LIBRARIAN

who fed this hungry young reader's love of books

when I was growing up. — TW

Text copyright © 2020 by Tracey West
Illustrations copyright © 2020 by Scholastic Inc.

Library of Congress Cataloging-in-Publication Data
Names: West, Tracey, 1965- author. | Loveridge, Matt. | West, Tracey, 1965- Dragon Masters ; 17.
Title: Fortress of the Stone Dragon / by Tracey West ; illustrated by Daniel Griffo.
Description: First edition. | New York : Branches/Scholastic Inc., 2020.
| Series: Dragon Masters ; 17 | Summary: Not all of the wizards who were freed from Maldred's time-trap were good wizards; one of them, Astrid, is planning on working a spell that will bring to life the bones that lie scattered in the Fortress of the Stone Dragon, bones that belonged to creatures much bigger than dragons—and when his friends are turned to stone it is up to Drake to find a way to save them, including his own dragon, Worm.
Identifiers: LCCN 2019036368 | ISBN 9781338540314 (paperback) |
ISBN 9781338540321 (library binding) | ISBN 9781338540338 (ebook)
Subjects: LCSH: Dragons—Juvenile fiction. | Magic—Juvenile fiction. | Wizards—Juvenile fiction. |
Adventure stories. | CYAC: Dragons—Fiction. | Magic—Fiction. | Wizards—Fiction. | Adventure and adventurers—Fiction. | LCGFT: Action and adventure fiction.
Classification: LCC PZ7.W51937 Fp 2020 | DDC 813.54 [Fic]—dc23
LC record available at https://lccn.loc.gov/2019036368

10 9 8 7 6 5 4 3 2   20 21 22 23 24

Printed in China   62

First edition, October 2020
Illustrated by Matt Loveridge
Edited by Katie Carella
Book design by Christian Zelaya

DRAGON MASTERS

FORTRESS OF THE STONE DRAGON

BY

TRACEY WEST

BRANCHES

SCHOLASTIC INC.

THE WIZARD SISTERS

We must be ready to fight!" said Mina, the Dragon Master from the Far North. The eight-year-old girl paced back and forth. She wore thick fur boots and had an ax tucked into her belt.

Drake, Bo, Rori, and Ana — the Dragon Masters of Bracken — were gathered around Mina. So was Eko, a Dragon Mage. Griffith, the royal wizard, was there, too. Mina had come a long way with Frost, her Ice Dragon. She had a message from her wizard, Hulda.

"Mina, what is Hulda's message?" Griffith asked.

"The trouble started when Drake and Rori released those wizards caught in a time spell," Mina began.

"Lukas and the Time Dragon helped us break the spell," Drake interrupted. "And Griffith was there, too."

Maldred, an evil wizard, had trapped his enemies in time. Some of the trapped wizards were good. And some were bad. But now they were all free.

"One of those wizards was Hulda's sister, Astrid. She is very dangerous," Mina warned. "Let Hulda tell you herself."

She turned to her pale blue dragon. "Frost! Magic Ice Mirror!"

Frost opened his mouth, and a sheet of ice formed. It hung in the air.

The face of a woman with fair blond hair appeared in the ice.

"Griffith, Dragon Masters, I need your help," Hulda said. "But first, let me tell you about my sister."

Hulda's face disappeared. A new face appeared — the face of Astrid. She looked like Hulda, but she had red hair.

"Astrid and I come from a long line of wizards," Hulda said. "We both gained magic powers when we were children. Astrid always tried to impress our parents by doing better magic than I could."

Rori interrupted. "That sounds like me and my sisters. We always race each other to see who is the fastest."

A picture of a castle high on a hill appeared in the ice mirror.

Hulda continued her story. "We both went to school in Belerion at the Castle of the Wizards. When we left, we went to the Far North Lands. I went to serve King Lars and Queen Sigrid. Astrid went to serve King Albin."

King Albin's face appeared in the ice mirror.

"One summer, the crops in King Albin's kingdom began to die," Hulda said. "Astrid used magic to save them. But King Albin took all the credit."

"That's not fair!" Rori said.

Hulda nodded. "This made Astrid very angry. I understood how she felt. But Astrid took it too far."

Astrid appeared in the ice mirror. She walked through a swirling cloud. Her eyes flashed with anger.

"Astrid cast a spell on King Albin. Donkey ears sprouted from his head," Hulda said. "King Albin was so angry! He asked me to undo the spell, and of course I did. Then he banished Astrid."

"He kicked her out of the kingdom?" Rori asked.

"Yes," Hulda said. "She begged the people of her kingdom to help her, but nobody did. I said she could live with me, but she refused. She was angry with me for helping King Albin."

"Where did Astrid go?" Ana asked.

"She roamed the world, studying on her own," Hulda replied. "Then one day, Astrid came to me. She had learned dark, terrible magic."

Drake held his breath.

"What did Astrid do next?" Bo asked.

Hulda answered him. "She put all of King Albin's kingdom under a sleeping spell!"

A DARK PLAN

na gasped. "What an awful thing for Astrid to do! Is everyone in King Albin's kingdom still asleep?"

"No," Mina replied. "But it took seventeen wizards to undo Astrid's powerful spell!"

The picture in the ice mirror changed again. Astrid walked through a rainstorm. Red magic flowed from her fingertips.

"My sister told me that she wanted to become a great wizard of dark magic," Hulda said. "The best in the world. She planned to steal Maldred's secrets. She asked me to join her, and I refused. That was the last I heard of her."

"She must have battled Maldred, and he trapped her in his time spell!" Drake said.

Hulda's face returned to the ice mirror.

"I have been tracking my sister in my gazing ball since she has been free," she explained. "Astrid has traveled the world collecting items that are very hard to find. I fear she is preparing to cast a very dangerous dark spell."

Five rare items appeared in the ice mirror. Griffith named them.

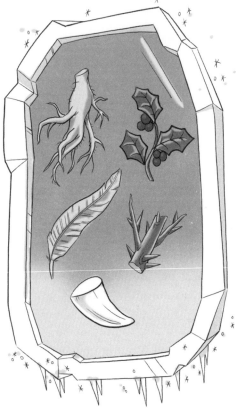

"One mandrake root," he said. "A sprig of black mistletoe. The tail feather of a ghost raven. A branch from a shadow bush. The tooth of a spirit bear."

"I am not sure what spell she is working on," Hulda said. "Griffith, do you know?"

"I do not," Griffith answered. "But Jayana, the Head Wizard, might."

"I must stay here in the Far North Lands," Hulda explained. "Once Astrid has what she needs, I worry she may come back here. She might try to cast another spell on King Albin's kingdom. I need to protect it."

Mina stepped forward. "Then I will go see Jayana," she said.

Griffith nodded. "Good idea. Drake can go with you."

"Thank you, all," Hulda said. Yellow sparks shot from her fingertips, and the ice mirror disappeared.

Bo turned to Griffith. "Should we go with Drake and Mina?"

Griffith shook his head. "I need you, Rori, and Ana to stay here with me and Eko," he said. "There are many evil wizards on the loose besides Astrid. We must be ready in case any of them start causing trouble."

The wizard turned and began to walk quickly. "Follow me, everyone!"

They followed Griffith to his workshop. He scribbled on a piece of paper.

"Mina, take this list of spell ingredients to Jayana at the Castle of the Wizards," he instructed, handing it to her. "Drake, get Worm to transport you there right away."

Griffith gave Drake a small mirror.

"Is this a magic mirror? Like the one you gave me when I went to the Naga's temple?" Drake asked.

"Yes," the wizard replied. "Use this to report to me after you talk to Jayana."

"Got it!" Drake said, and he tucked the mirror into his belt.

"Good luck, Drake and Mina! And hurry!" Ana said.

"Yes!" Bo added. "Find out what Astrid is planning so we can stop her!"

GRIFFITH'S WORKSHOP

THE CASTLE OF THE WIZARDS

rake and Mina rushed out of Griffith's workshop. Drake patted his Earth Dragon, Worm.

"Worm, can you please transport us to Belerion?" Drake asked.

Drake wore a green Dragon Stone around his neck. It started to glow.

He heard Worm's voice inside his head.

Yes, the dragon replied.

Drake nodded to Mina. "Do you remember how this works?"

"I touch Frost with one hand and Worm with the other," Mina said, placing one hand on each dragon. "Then *whoosh!* We're gone."

"Right," Drake said. "Worm, take us to the Castle of the Wizards!"

Green light flashed. Drake's stomach flip-flopped.

The light faded. They appeared at the gates of the castle.

The wizard guard frowned. "Halt!" she cried. "There are no dragons allowed inside the castle."

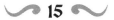

"If you do not let us in, we will storm your castle!" Mina said. She put her hand on her ax handle.

"It's okay, Mina. Worm and Frost can stay here," Drake said. He turned to the guard. "We will leave our dragons outside. But Mina and I need to see the Head Wizard right away! We're here on important wizard business for Griffith of the Green Fields."

"Very well," the guard said. She opened the gate. "You will find her at the end of the hallway."

Drake and Mina dashed into the castle. They quickly reached the door to the Head Wizard's workshop.

The door magically swung open. A wizard with white hair and a wrinkled face smiled at them.

"Drake! Mina! Come in!" Jayana called out.

The Dragon Masters entered the room.

"Jayana!" Drake cried. "It's so good to see you! We need your help!"

Mina passed her the piece of paper with the spell ingredients written on it.

The Head Wizard looked at the list. She frowned. "These are the ingredients for a very dark spell," she said. "I hope Griffith isn't making this!"

"No! Astrid the wizard has collected these items," Mina said.

"I knew Astrid," Jayana said. "There is no dark magic that she would not try."

"Do you know what kind of spell these ingredients are for?" Drake asked.

Jayana looked worried. "Yes. These items are only ever mixed together in one thing: a False Life spell. It is used to bring to life things that are not alive. Like rocks, or wood, or bones."

Drake shivered. "That sounds creepy."

"Yes," Jayana agreed. "I fear that Astrid may be planning something terrible!"

JAYANA'S GAZING BALL

We must stop Astrid from casting the False Life spell!" Mina cried.

Jayana walked over to her gazing ball.

"Let's see where Astrid is right now," she said. Magic flowed from her fingers.

The ball glowed with silver light.

A picture appeared inside it. Drake saw Astrid riding a horse across a desert.

"Those are the red sands of Navid. And that is Mount Ruby behind her. But what is she doing there?" Jayana asked. Then she frowned. "Unless..."

"Unless what?" Mina asked.

"Unless she is heading to the Fortress of the Stone Dragon," Jayana said.

"Why would she go there?" Drake asked.

"That fortress is the most magical place in Navid," Jayana said. "It looks like she is about two days away."

Drake remembered the mirror in his belt. He looked into the mirror. "Griffith?" he asked.

The wizard's face appeared. "Drake! What have you found out?"

"I'll let Jayana explain," Drake said, and he handed the mirror to the Head Wizard.

Jayana told Griffith what they had learned.

Griffith frowned. "A False Life spell," he said. "Is there any magic powerful enough to undo it?"

"I don't think so," Jayana said. "I will have my top wizards work on it. The spell takes very long to create, so we will have time"

"I'll see what I can learn from my books," Griffith said. "In the meantime, Drake and Mina, go to the fortress. Warn the Dragon Master there that Astrid is on her way."

Then the magic mirror went dark.

"Let's go!" Mina said — and then she yawned. That made Drake yawn, too.

Jayana looked out the window. A bright moon hung in the sky.

"There is time for you and your dragons to rest and eat," Jayana said. "Worm can transport you to the fortress in the morning. You will still be at least one day ahead of Astrid."

"Sleep would be nice," Drake said.

"I do not need rest," Mina said, but she yawned again. She didn't argue when Jayana led them to the guest quarters.

The wizards fed Worm and Frost. They brought Drake and Mina soup and bread.

The Dragon Masters and their dragons got a good night's sleep.

Jayana met them at the dragon stable in the morning.

"My wizards and I will join you soon. But first, we need to find magic strong enough to fight Astrid," she told Drake and Mina. "If Astrid gets there before we do, hide! Do not approach her on your own. She is dangerous."

"I am from the Land of the Far North," Mina said. "We do not hide."

"Be careful, Mina," Jayana said. "And safe travels to you all!"

Jayana waved as Worm transported Drake, Mina, and Frost to the Fortress of the Stone Dragon in Navid. When they got there, Drake felt the heat from the desert sand through his shoes. He squinted and looked up at the sturdy fortress. He counted eight tall towers, joined by high stone walls.

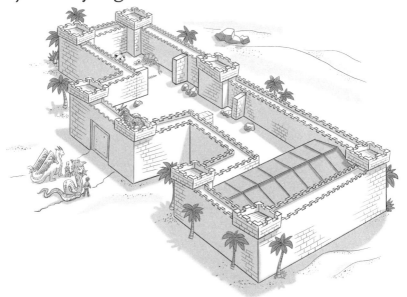

A voice rang out from the nearest tower. "Who goes there?"

INTO THE FORTRESS

I am Drake, and this is my dragon, Worm!"
Drake called out. His voice echoed across the
stone fortress.

"And I am Mina of the Far North. This is
my dragon, Frost!" Mina announced.

"Can we come in? We are friendly. We are
here with a warning!" Drake said.

"How do I know you're telling the truth?" the voice replied. Drake shaded his eyes as he looked toward the far-right tower. He saw a boy with dark hair. A green Dragon Stone glittered around the boy's neck.

"We are Dragon Masters, just like you are," Drake replied. He held up his own Dragon Stone to show him.

The boy frowned. "How can I be sure that you are friendly?"

Beside the boy, Drake saw a tall gray dragon.

That must be the Stone Dragon, Drake thought. He called up to the boy, "Worm will tell your dragon that we mean no harm."

"Have Worm do it, then!" the boy cried.

Drake turned to Worm. "Please tell the Stone Dragon that we are not going to cause any trouble."

Worm gazed up at the dragon. After a moment, Drake saw the boy's Dragon Stone glow. His dragon was communicating with him.

The boy slowly nodded. "Shaka says I can trust you. I will let you in."

The boy and dragon disappeared from the tower. Drake heard a groan in front of them as the stone door slowly began to slide to the side.

The Dragon Master from the tower waited for them. Next to him, Shaka's body was glowing with gray energy. The stone door seemed to be sliding on its own.

Is the Stone Dragon moving the door with her powers? Drake wondered.

Then he, Mina, Worm, and Frost stepped into the fortress. Drake got a good look at Shaka. She had a strong, sturdy shape. Her gray scales reminded him of stones. The sharp spikes going down her back looked like dark crystals.

The Stone Dragon began to glow again, and the door slid closed behind them.

"Whoa!" Drake cried. "Can Shaka move things with her mind? Worm, my Earth Dragon, can do that."

"Shaka can connect to anything made of stone," the boy replied, and he smiled for the first time. "I am Caspar."

"Jayana, the Head Wizard, told us that this place is very magical," Drake said.

"It is," Caspar said. "Let me show you the Garden of the Beasts."

They followed Caspar across a courtyard. Giant rocks rose up from the ground. Some of the rocks were bigger than the dragons.

Caspar led them into a different courtyard. Scattered across the ground were bones. Hundreds of bones. And the bones were huge. Some of them were as long as Worm, and as thick as a tree trunk!

Drake and Mina gasped.

"Bones!" Mina said. "Do you think that . . ."

"Astrid is going to bring these bones to life!" Drake cried.

THE GARDEN OF THE BEASTS

Drake and Mina stared at each other in shock.

"Who is Astrid?" Caspar asked.

"We came here to warn you about her," Drake said. "Astrid is an evil wizard. She's working on a spell that can bring things to life."

"That sounds impossible!" Caspar cried.

"Tell us about these bones," Mina said. "What kind of creatures have bones as big as these? Are they dragons?"

"These are the bones of giant beasts that lived long ago. Long before humans and probably even before dragons," Caspar replied. "Come."

Caspar walked them over to one of the walls. "These are paintings of the beasts. Of what we think they looked like."

Drake studied the pictures. Some of the beasts had very long necks. Others had long tails. Some walked on two legs. Some walked on four legs.

"They kind of look like dragons," Drake said.

"They do," Caspar said. "But many of the beasts were much bigger than dragons. And we do not know what powers they had."

"They look strong and dangerous," Mina said. "Astrid would probably use them to do terrible things. Caspar, we must prepare for her attack!"

"This fortress is made of stone. Nobody can get in here unless Shaka opens the door," Caspar said. "Shaka can crush things. She can make the earth shake. And she has a secret power that she can use in an emergency."

"Astrid is a very powerful evil wizard," Drake said.

"Not more powerful than Shaka," Caspar boasted.

"I must tell Hulda that we know what Astrid is planning," Mina said. "Frost, create an ice —"

Boom!

They heard a loud noise outside the fortress.

"To the tower!" Caspar cried. He and Shaka climbed to the top of the nearest tower.

Worm transported Drake, Mina, and Frost there. They all looked down at the scene outside the fortress and gasped.

"It's an army!" Drake cried.

ASTRID'S ARMY

Down below, a huge swirling portal of red energy had opened up in front of the fortress. An army of men and women wearing armor marched out of it. The soldiers carried shields, bows, and arrows. And behind them, floating above the ground, was Astrid!

"How did she get here so fast?" Mina asked. "Jayana said she was at least one day away."

"She must have created a magic portal to take a shortcut," Drake guessed. "And it looks like she picked up some soldiers on the way."

"She can bring all the soldiers she wants," Caspar said. "Nobody can break into this fortress!"

More soldiers came out of the portal. They marched in straight lines toward the fortress. Some pushed weapons on wheels.

"What are those wagons?" Mina asked.

"They're called catapults, and they throw rocks," Drake replied. "Jean, the Dragon Master of the Silver Dragon, uses them to protect her castle."

Remembering Jean, Drake reached for the silver sword she had given him.

I wish I had taken some sword-fighting lessons from Jean, he thought. *But one sword won't stop this army. We need wizards!*

He took the magic mirror from his belt.

"I will let Griffith know we need help," he said. Drake looked into the mirror. "Griffith! It's Drake! Astrid is —"

Wham! An arrow slammed into the mirror, knocking it out of Drake's hands.

It smashed onto the stone floor.

Drake picked up his mirror. The glass had shattered.

"No!" Drake cried. He turned to Mina and Caspar. "Jayana told us we should hide if we saw Astrid."

"We must fight Astrid now!" Mina said.

"Shaka and I will not back down," Caspar said. "It is our duty to protect this fortress!"

The soldiers stopped marching. They all drew their arrows at once. Drake noticed for the first time that their eyes were glazed over red. But Astrid's eyes were clear. She walked to the front of the army, wearing a glowing red crystal around her neck.

She's controlling the soldiers, he realized.

Mina saw it, too. "The soldiers can't help what they are doing," she said. "Astrid is controlling them. Just like Vasty the Ice Giant used a blue crystal to control Frost."

"I remember!" Drake said.

"I had to destroy the crystal to undo the spell," Mina added.

"Exactly! So it's not fair to attack the soldiers," Drake said. "We need to destroy Astrid's red crystal to stop her. But it's too risky. We should hide!"

"We don't have to hide," Mina argued. "Frost can freeze Astrid from up here. Then I can grab the crystal and crush it with my ax."

"That is a good plan," Caspar agreed.

Astrid gazed up at the tower. A slow grin spread across her face as her eyes locked with Mina's.

Then she turned to her soldiers. "Attack!" she yelled.

ARROWS AND ROCKS

Whoosh! A shower of arrows flew at the fortress.

"Worm, stop the arrows!" Drake yelled.

Worm's body glowed bright green, and the arrows froze in midair. Then they dropped to the ground.

"Yes, Drake!" Caspar cheered.

More soldiers poured through the portal. They sent another wave of arrows flying through the air.

"Frost, freeze the arrows with your ice breath!" Mina commanded, as her Dragon Stone glowed.

The Ice Dragon opened his mouth and shot a blast of shimmering, sparkling air off the tower.

The freezing blast froze the next wave of arrows. Covered in ice, they fell to the ground with a clatter.

"Good move!" Drake said.

Below, some soldiers got ready to fire another round of arrows. Drake saw other soldiers launching the catapults. The catapult baskets lunged forward, shooting rocks at the fortress.

"Worm, stop those rocks!" Drake cried.

Worm glowed green again. He focused his mind powers on the rocks. Like the arrows, the rocks dropped to the ground. The soldiers scrambled to pick up their fallen arrows so they could attack again.

"Nice work, Drake!" Mina said. "Frost, freeze Astrid!"

The Ice Dragon reared his head back. He opened his mouth.

Then he closed it again.

"Frost, what's wrong?" Mina asked. Her Dragon Stone glowed. "Drake, Frost says he can't see Astrid!"

Drake looked down below. The wizard was gone.

Then Drake heard Worm's voice in his head. *I sense danger down by the door.*

"We need to get to the door!" Drake cried. "Mina, keep watch. Worm, transport!"

Drake and Worm transported down into the fortress. A moment later, Shaka ran up behind them, with Caspar on her back.

"Nobody will get inside while Shaka is here," Caspar said. "Do not worry, Drake."

Just then, Shaka let out a roar.

Rooowwwwwwwwr!

The stone door was pulsing with red, wavy energy!

BATTLE AT THE FORTRESS

tand back from the door! That is dark magic!" Drake yelled. He pointed to the glimmering red door.

Just then, Mina and Frost flew down and landed beside Worm.

"We couldn't see Astrid from the tower, so we flew out to find her," Mina said. "She's right on the other side of that door!"

"We know. She is casting some kind of spell," Drake said. "Look!"

The Dragon Masters and their dragons watched with wide eyes as the strong, stone door slowly disappeared.

"This can't be happening!" Caspar cried.

Outside, Astrid stood where the door had been, grinning. Red energy sparked from her fingertips. Behind her, the soldiers were ready to shoot their weapons again.

"You cannot stop us, children," she said. "Move aside and nobody will get hurt."

Shaka stomped her feet.

"We will never let you in," Caspar said.

Astrid stepped forward. Drake noticed something then. The evil wizard had tiny, glowing bottles tucked into loops on her belt. Each bottle held a different color liquid.

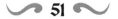

What are those for? he wondered.

Astrid moved to the side. "You give me no choice, then," she said. "Army, attack!"

The soldiers let their arrows fly.

"Quick, Worm! Stop the arrows again!" Drake commanded.

Worm glowed green. Suddenly, the arrows stopped in midair. Then they dropped to the ground.

"Shaka, forward!" Caspar yelled, and the Stone Dragon charged toward the army.

"Drake and Caspar, keep Worm and Shaka focused on those soldiers!" Mina called out. "Frost and I will take care of Astrid! We must destroy her red crystal!"

Drake was worried that Shaka might hurt the soldiers. But she didn't. Instead, the Stone Dragon stomped on the catapults, crushing them.

The soldiers reloaded their arrows. Their eyes still glowed red from Astrid's magic.

Then an idea hit Drake. He knew that Worm could break up big rocks with his mind powers. Why not a crystal?

"Worm, can you use your powers to break Astrid's red crystal?" he asked.

I will try, Worm replied.

Drake looked at Astrid. The evil wizard was throwing red magic blasts at Frost. But the blasts couldn't hit the Ice Dragon. She was flying too fast.

Worm glowed green. The crystal started to shake. Frowning, Astrid looked down.

Poof! The red crystal exploded into dust.

The soldiers stopped fighting. They looked confused.

The wizard turned to Drake, furious. "How *dare* you?" she asked.

Mina and Frost swooped down behind Astrid. "Frost, freeze her!"

Astrid grabbed a bottle of bright orange liquid from her belt. She quickly swallowed it as she turned to face Frost.

"What are you waiting for, dragon?" she asked. "Hit me with your best shot!"

The Ice Dragon aimed a blast of freezing air at the wizard. It trapped her in a block of ice!

FIRE!

"Good work, Frost!" Mina cheered. The dragon landed next to Astrid's frozen body.

Some of the soldiers ran back into the portal as it closed. Others ran off into the desert.

Caspar hopped off Shaka. He walked around the frozen block of ice containing Astrid. "I am glad you two showed up," he said. "I must now admit that the fortress was not as safe as I thought."

"But it is safe now," Mina said. "And Jayana should be here soon. She will know what to do with this frozen wizard."

Something was bothering Drake. "What if Astrid uses magic to unfreeze herself before Jayana gets here?"

"Remember that time when Hulda got frozen? She could not get out," Mina said. "I don't think wizards can perform magic when they're frozen."

Drake nodded. "That makes sense."

Suddenly, an orange glow came from inside the block of ice.

"Look!" Drake said, pointing.

"Oh no!" Mina said. "Everybody, get back, quickly!"

Drake touched Worm, and they transported to safety behind one of the big rocks. Mina and Frost flew up and landed next to them. Caspar climbed onto Shaka's back.

"Stone Dragons are not afraid of wizards," he said. "Let us see what Astrid will do."

Whoosh! A stream of fire burst through the block of ice, melting it.

Astrid floated out, and Drake gasped.

The wizard was breathing fire, just like a Fire Dragon!

ASTRID'S PLAN

Shaka stomped toward Astrid, with Caspar on her back. The wizard shot a stream of fire at the Stone Dragon.

Caspar laughed. "Fire cannot hurt Shaka."

"No, but it can hurt *you*!" Astrid said. She hurled another stream of fire at him.

Shaka glowed. A flat piece of stone flew up from the ground and stopped the fire stream from hitting Caspar.

"Nice try," Caspar said. "You may shoot fire like a dragon, but you are no dragon."

"I am smarter than a dragon," she replied. "A wizard named Maldred taught me how to steal dragon powers. But I do it better. I figured out how to *use* them!"

She patted the bottles on her belt.

Drake nudged Mina. "There must be all different dragon powers in those bottled liquids," he whispered. "The orange liquid gave her the power of a Fire Dragon."

Astrid floated higher up and landed on a big rock. Caspar and Shaka stomped closer to her.

"How long does each dragon power last?" Caspar asked.

"Only for a short time," Astrid replied. "But it doesn't matter. I have captured the powers of eight dragons so far. When one power wears out, I can use another one."

"I don't care if you have the power of one hundred dragons!" Caspar said. "Shaka and I will defend this fortress. Leave here now!"

Astrid shook her head. "You are a brave little boy. But you are not good at listening. Didn't you hear me? I will drain your dragon's powers unless *you* leave this fortress. Now get out of my way! I have a spell to cast."

"We know your plan with the Garden of the Beasts," Caspar said. "You want to bring those bones back to life!"

Astrid smiled. "Maybe you are smarter than I thought," she said. "Yes, that is my plan. Then no army will be able to defeat me! I will conquer the Land of the Far North. And then . . . the world!"

"You will never rule this kingdom!" Caspar cried.

"Princess Daria leads us, and she is strong and brave!"

"Ha!" Astrid cried, and flames flickered from her lips. "Wizards are more powerful than any normal human. *We* should be running things!"

While Astrid had been talking with Caspar, Drake whispered to Mina, "Astrid is distracted. We could try a surprise attack. But what can we do?"

"Could Worm break that big rock she's standing on to throw her off balance?" Mina suggested. "Astrid's fire power should wear off soon. Then Frost could freeze her again."

"Good plan!" Drake said. "I'll wait for the right time..."

Mina nodded. Then she suddenly jumped out from their hiding place and began to argue with Astrid.

"Wizards should *not* rule!" Mina said. "They have too much power, and too much power is dangerous. Hulda taught me that."

"Hulda!" Astrid's eyes flashed. But this time, no fire came from her mouth as she spoke. "Did my sister send you here? No matter. I caught her spying on me through her gazing ball yesterday, and I taught her a lesson."

Mina clenched her fists. "What did you do to Hulda?" she yelled.

Drake closed his eyes. He sent a message to Worm.

Worm, break the big rock Astrid is standing on!

Worm started glowing. The rock under Astrid's feet began to shake. Red sparks shot from her fingertips. But before she could cast a spell, the rock broke into pieces.

Astrid fell and her head smacked the ground. She stopped moving.

Mina jumped on Frost. "Freeze Astrid, now!" she commanded.

Caspar's Dragon Stone began to glow.

"No! I've got this!" Caspar shouted to Mina. Then he turned to his dragon. "Shaka, use your secret power!" he yelled.

CHAPTER 12

THE SECRET POWER

haka roared, ready to attack Astrid. The wizard was just starting to open her eyes.

"Wait!" Drake shouted as he and Worm rushed out from behind their rock.

Shaka looked at Caspar, confused.

"Just one moment, Shaka," Caspar told his dragon.

"What does the secret power do?" Drake asked.

"Shaka can turn people into stone," Caspar replied.

Drake gasped. "You mean, like statues?"

Caspar nodded. "Yes. It is a very dangerous power. That is why it can only be used in an emergency. But Astrid must be stopped."

"I agree," Mina said. "Give the command, Caspar."

Caspar patted Shaka's neck. "NOW!"

Gray beams shot from Shaka's eyes. But Astrid jumped up and her hand flew to her belt. She grabbed an empty bottle. Red magic flowed from her hands and made the bottle glow. She held it in front of her.

"*Captivatis!*" she cried.

The gray beams flowed inside the bottle.

"Caspar, call off the attack!" Drake yelled.

But it was too late. Shiny gray liquid had filled the bottle. Astrid gulped it down. Her eyes began to glow with gray light, just as Shaka's eyes had glowed.

Caspar's eyes were wide with fear. Shaka stomped away from Astrid, but Drake knew the big dragon couldn't escape fast enough.

Mina and Frost launched into the air. "Frost, freeze her!" Mina yelled.

Frost glowed, building up power for his ice attack.

Drake touched Worm. "Transport us next to Shaka! Then transport us all out of here!"

But Astrid moved fast. Faster than Frost. Faster than Worm. Gray beams shot from Astrid's eyes.

Drake and Worm appeared next to Caspar and Shaka.

"No!" Drake cried.

Caspar and his dragon had already been turned into stone!

WATCH OUT!

Drake stared at Caspar and Shaka in shock. They were statues. It looked like they had been carved out of stone.

Overhead, Frost shot an ice blast at Astrid. The wizard dodged it. Then she aimed gray energy beams at Drake.

"Drake, watch out!" Mina cried from above.

Drake turned to see Astrid shooting beams from her eyes. He ducked behind Worm as his Earth Dragon powered up with energy.

Mina and Frost swooped down just as Astrid's attack hit a wall of green energy in front of Worm.

"Astrid! Stop this at once!" Mina called out as Frost slammed into the wizard.

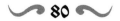

Astrid fell backward. As she fell, the beams from her eyes changed direction. They zapped Frost!

Mina and Frost turned to stone in front of Drake's eyes. They hit the ground with a thud.

Then Astrid turned to Drake.

"No!" he cried. Drake's mind raced. *I need to help my friends. But I can't help them if Worm and I are turned to stone.*

He put his hand on Worm.

"Worm, transport us right outside the fortress!" Drake said.

They transported in a flash, landing in the hot desert sand.

Drake let go of Worm and tried to think. *I don't want to leave Mina and Caspar. But I don't know how to help them. Why haven't Jayana and the other wizards arrived yet?*

He looked up at Worm. His dragon wasn't moving. Then Drake saw it. A gray glow was slowly spreading across Worm's body.

"Worm, no!" Drake yelled.

Drake heard laughter. Astrid stepped out of the fortress. She gazed up at Worm as he turned to stone.

"Your dragon will be a nice statue outside *my* fortress," she said, smiling. "A warning to anyone who tries to stop me."

Then she looked at Drake. "And of course I'll need a sad little boy statue, too."

Her eyes glowed with gray light.

Drake turned to run, and a light flashed in front of him.

Poof! Hulda appeared. She saw the stone statues of Mina, Frost, Caspar, Shaka, and Worm. Her eyes grew wide.

Astrid gasped. "Sister!" she cried. Then she laughed again. "Have you come to stop me?"

"I *will* stop you, Astrid, but not today," she said. She wrapped her arms around Drake.

Poof! Hulda and Drake disappeared.

CHAPTER 14

THREE DRAGONS

Hulda and Drake appeared in the Head Wizard's workshop in Belerion. Jayana and five other wizards were gathered around her desk.

"Get Drake some tea, quickly," Jayana said.

She hurried to Drake and led him to a chair. She snapped her fingers and a soft blanket appeared on his lap. Then a wizard handed him a cup of warm tea.

Drake's hands shook as he lifted the cup to his lips.

"Drake, I am sorry," Jayana said. "I should have guessed that Astrid would use a magic portal to get to the fortress faster. I didn't realize her powers were as strong as they are."

"I would have gotten there sooner, too, but Astrid delayed me with a binding spell that she sent through my gazing ball," Hulda said. "As soon as I got free, I came."

Drake swallowed some tea.

"Astrid is going to bring the Garden of the Beasts to life," he said. "She wants to rule the world. We tried to stop her, but . . . Mina and Frost, and Caspar and Shaka, and Worm . . ."

Tears welled up in Drake's eyes.

"My sister turned them all into stone," Hulda finished for him.

The Head Wizard held his hand. "Oh, Drake, I am sorry this has happened," she said.

"How did Astrid do it?" Hulda asked.

Drake told them all about the bottles of dragon powers on her belt.

"She stole Shaka's power and then used it to turn everyone into stone," he explained.

"Do not worry, Drake," Jayana said. "We will save your friends. We will stop Astrid."

Hulda looked at Jayana like she didn't believe her.

"It will not be easy," Jayana admitted. "My wizards and I have had no luck finding a way to reverse the False Life spell. But what has Griffith found out?"

Drake held up his broken mirror. "I haven't been able to contact him," he said.

Jayana smiled. "That is easily fixed," she said. She waved her hand over the mirror, and a silver glow hit the glass. She handed it back to Drake, and the mirror's surface was smooth again.

"Thank you," Drake said. Then he called into the mirror. "Griffith!"

"Drake!" Griffith said. "Are you all right?"

"Not really," Drake said. Thinking of his friends and their dragons, he almost started to cry again.

Jayana took the mirror from him and explained everything to Griffith. Then she gave the mirror back to Drake.

"Drake, we can help everyone who has been turned to stone," Griffith promised. "And Ana has found a way to reverse the False Life spell."

Ana appeared in the mirror. "Drake! On a hunch, I flew to the Dragon Temple in the Land of Pyramids. It turns out, dragons are the key to breaking the spell."

"What did you find out?" Drake asked, sitting up straight.

"We will need to find three special dragons," Ana told him. "We must look for them right away!"

"Yes! But . . . how can I go anywhere without Worm?" Drake asked.

Suddenly, Drake's Dragon Stone began to glow. He heard Worm's voice inside his head.

Drake, where are you?

TRACEY WEST likes writing about dragons and wizards. She uses her imagination to come up with their powers. When it came time to create a new evil wizard, she imagined how powerful a wizard with dragon powers might be.

Tracey is the stepmom to three grown-up kids. She shares her home with her husband, one cat, two dogs, and a bunch of chickens. They live in the misty mountains of New York state, where it is easy to imagine dragons roaming free in the green hills.

MATT LOVERIDGE loves illustrating children's books. When he's not painting or drawing, he likes hiking, biking, and drinking milk right from the carton. He lives in the mountains of Utah with his wife and kids, and their black dog named Blue.

DRAGON MASTERS
FORTRESS OF THE STONE DRAGON

Questions and Activities

Astrid was banished from the Far North Lands. Why was she sent away?

Shaka is a Stone Dragon who can use her mind to move things made of stone. But she also has a secret power . . . What is this power?

Mina and Drake decide not to attack Astrid's soldiers, even though her soldiers are attacking them. Why do they make this decision? Reread pages 41–43.

Astrid collected five ingredients for her False Life spell. Make a list of the ingredients.

The bones in the Garden of the Beasts belonged to real creatures that lived on Earth long ago. Draw what you think these creatures looked like—and give them powers!